Welcome to the world of Beast Quest!

When a series of Beast attacks shocked the peaceful land of Tangala, Queen Aroha called for a worthy Master or Mistress of the Beasts. But one fighter wasn't enough for the grave danger the kingdom faced, and four candidates pledged their weapons to the Queen to restore peace. There is strength in unity and power in friendship. Together, Katya from the Forest of Shadows, Nolan of Aran, Miandra from the western shore and Rafe of Pania will venture to new lands and battle enemies of the realm. The fate of Tangala is in their hands.

While there's blood in their veins, the New Protectors will never give up the Quest…

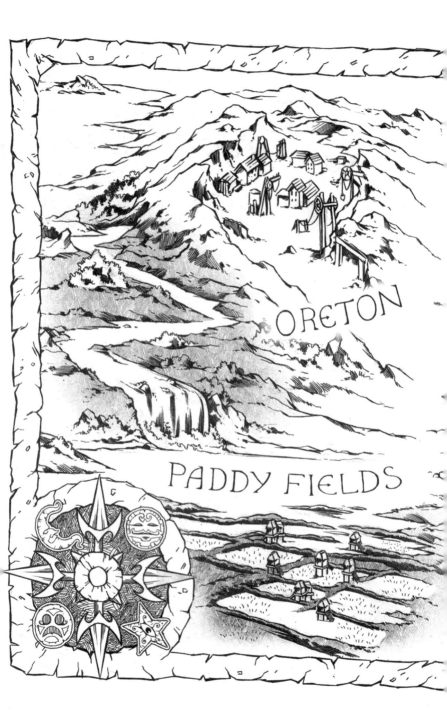

ORETON

PADDY FIELDS

There are special gold coins to collect in this book. You will earn one coin for every chapter you read.

Find out what to do with your coins at the end of the book.

CONTENTS

It's good to be back!

Tom may have freed the Tangalan brats, but my games with them are only just beginning.

Now I have escaped my prison kingdom, I will have my vengeance. I have summoned forth from the Netherworld four creatures to terrorise Tangala. And this time, there'll be no Master of the Beasts to come to their aid.

Let's see how these four 'heroes' fair without their champion!

Malvel

RETURNING TO THE HOMESTEAD

Needles of dread pricked Nolan's skin as he stared into the magical portal before him. The swirling green and gold patterns churned sickeningly.

A short while ago Nolan had been wolfing down his porridge, dressed in his smartest tunic, full of excitement for the ceremony to come. Now he wished he'd skipped breakfast. It sat in his gut like a heavy lump of iron. He looked at the scythe in his hand. The weapon's edge gleamed gold,

polished to a high shine. Tom had just sacrificed some of his own magical strength to enhance the power of the new heroes' weapons, making each one now as light as a feather. *What if I'm not worthy?* thought Nolan. *What if I let him down?*

He glanced at Tom, who lay nearby on the royal dais, his eyes closed and his chest barely rising and falling. Nolan straightened his spine. *I will be ready. For Tom. For Tangala.*

Nolan and his three new friends, Katya, Miandra and Rafe, had all just been appointed Tangala's apprentice Masters and Mistresses of the Beasts, the New Protectors of the Kingdom. For Nolan, it was a chance to prove himself to his father, to make his family proud. But during the ceremony, Tom, Avantia's Master of the Beasts, had been poisoned by the Evil Wizard Malvel. Now Tom's recovery depended on Nolan, Katya,

Rafe and Miandra each recovering a magical ingredient scattered to one of the four corners of Tangala. But to retrieve the ingredients, they would first have to defeat a Beast.

"We'd better get going now if we're to help Tom," Queen Aroha said from Nolan's side. Jolted from his thoughts, a hot blush spread up Nolan's cheeks.

"Of course, Your Majesty, I'm so sorry," he said, bowing low.

Aroha put a hand on his shoulder. "Relax," she said. Her face was lined with sorrow, but she smiled wryly. "We're partners now. We won't get anywhere if you keep stopping to bow."

"Yes, Your Majesty," Nolan said, just

catching himself before he dropped into another bow.

"Better," Aroha said, still smiling. "Now, follow me." The Queen turned to the portal and stepped forwards, instantly vanishing with a shimmer of gold. After taking a deep breath, Nolan followed...

"Whoa!" His heart leapt as he pitched forwards, tumbling into empty space. A strong wind howled in his ears, and gold and green lights whirled around him. Suddenly, his feet hit the earth with a soft jolt, and everything went still. Nolan blinked and found himself looking out over the rolling green hills of Mylantis.

Familiar sweeping terraces of

young wheat rose on either side of them, bathed in hazy sunlight. The air smelled of rich, warm soil.

"I'm home!" Nolan exclaimed to Aroha. The palace with its gilded tapestries and marble flagstones already seemed like a distant memory. He turned just in time to see the portal shrink to a tiny spark, then vanish.

"I'd almost forgotten how peaceful it is here!" Aroha said, running her gaze over the hills with their soft green shoots and rising mist. Birdsong filled the air, but otherwise, it was quiet. "At least there's no sign of a Beast yet," she said.

Nolan pointed to a narrow track

that led up the nearest hill, winding back and forth between the stepped terraces. "My father's house is up there," Nolan told Aroha. "He's an elder in the village. He will know if anything strange has happened."

Aroha nodded. "Lead the way."

Almost as soon as he began to

climb, Nolan wished he was wearing his farming clothes and moccasins. Sticky mud sucked at his boots and beneath his scratchy tunic, beads of sweat rolled down his spine. He glanced back at the Queen, who was trudging through the mud in her full-dress armour, her face already flushed with heat.

"Would you prefer to take a less muddy route, Your Majesty?" he asked her. "Or I could fetch a donkey?"

Aroha arched an eyebrow. "I'm used to the trials of war, remember. A bit of mud isn't going to bother me. And don't call me 'Your Majesty'. If people find out who I am, it will complicate everything."

Nolan felt himself flushing again. "I'm so sorry," he said, dipping his head.

"And stop apologising!" Aroha laughed.

"I'll try!" Nolan said. But he couldn't help thinking that anyone who saw the Queen would know her at once. Nobody in Mylantis wore armour. Or carried a spear.

They climbed steadily onwards, passing small homesteads raised on stilts with chickens pecking around outside. The occasional cow lifted its eyes to them, then went back to grazing. Everything seemed so peaceful and normal that Nolan wondered if maybe they had come to the wrong place. Surely there would be some sign if a Beast was in Mylantis!

Eventually, Nolan's own home came into sight – a large, oblong farmhouse surrounded by vegetable plots and a few stilted outbuildings. Smoke rose from the chimney, and as they drew closer, Nolan spotted two familiar figures busy hoeing outside – his brothers, Riko and Boras. Their broad muscles strained beneath their tunics as they turned the soil.

"Hello!" Nolan called, lifting a hand.

His brothers turned. Riko scowled and Boras narrowed his eyes, his mouth a flat, angry line. "Finally come back to do your share on the farm, have you?" Riko asked.

"Looks more like he's off to a fancy-dress party," Boras muttered. "What are you wearing?" he asked Nolan. "And who's the knight in shining armour? Don't think she'll save you from father's temper!"

Riko smirked. "You're in big trouble, little brother," he said. "I'd turn back while you still can."

"I can't turn back," Nolan cried. "I'm here to warn you. A Beast is coming!"

Boras rolled his eyes. "Go tell Father. We're too busy working to listen to fairy stories." With that, Nolan's brothers went back to their hoeing.

Nolan turned away, his heart heavy.

"Those are your brothers?" Aroha asked, once they were out of earshot. "You don't look like them at all. And I'm glad to say you don't share their manners."

Nolan shrugged. "It's my fault they're angry," he said. "While I've been gone, they've had to do all my chores. I'll never be as big or strong as they are, so I'm not much use on the farm. They take after my mother."

"In that case, I should ask her to join my guard," Aroha quipped. "I'm always on the lookout for warrior women."

Nolan smiled sadly, the familiar pang of grief as painful as ever. "She passed away when I was little," he said. "I don't remember her well, but she was brave. I'm sure she would have made a good guard."

Aroha's face fell. "I'm so sorry," she said.

"It's all right," Nolan said, trying to keep his voice bright. "I wish she could see me now though, on a Quest with the Queen!"

They trudged on through the yard. Though the farmhouse windows were shuttered, the door stood open. Remembering his brother's warning, Nolan took a deep breath before leading Aroha inside.

The dusky kitchen was deserted, but a pot of stew bubbled on the stove. "Father?" Nolan called. A gruff groan, followed by the tap tap of a walking stick, answered him. A moment later his father, Dillan, stepped into the room, leaning heavily on his cane. A wave of guilt and sorrow washed over Nolan at the sight. His father had always been slight, but now a lifetime of toiling under the sun had bent and wasted his frame until his skin clung to his bones like parchment. His dark eyes were still sharp though, and his scowl was as fierce as ever as he jabbed a finger at Nolan's scythe.

"It's about time you returned to help your brothers!" Dillan snapped. "And at least you've brought the scythe back. Put it to work for once. Your fancy guest can make herself useful too, or she can be off. I don't much care which."

"But Father, I've come to warn you," Nolan tried. "There's a Beast coming to Mylantis. The town is in danger."

"I've no time for your nonsense," Dillan said. "There's wheat to take to town, or there'll be no bread for supper. You can help Valen with that if you've nothing better to do."

"But, Father, there really is a Beast coming!" Nolan tried again.

"All the more reason to get the wheat milled while we can," Dillan said. He lifted his walking cane and stabbed it towards the door. "Go on! Both of you."

Queen Aroha cast Nolan a sympathetic look, then turned to leave. Nolan followed behind her.

Outside, he ran both hands over his face. "What now?" Nolan asked Aroha.

"I guess we head to town, as your father said," she told him. "Maybe someone there will listen."

1

IN THE VILLAGE

Frustration burned inside Nolan
as he led Aroha towards the barn.
Inside, he found his other brother,
Valen, heaving a sack of grain on to
their cart. Their old donkey, Obie,
was already harnessed.

"Nolan!" Valen cried, his face
lighting up. Valen was a year older
than Nolan, and more than a head

taller, but still had the smooth, rounded cheeks of a boy. Unlike the rest of the family, he had always admired Nolan's dreams of becoming a hero. "I'm so glad you're back," Valen said, grinning. "Now Riko and Boras can boss you around instead of me!"

Nolan grinned back. Despite his worries, it was good to finally get a warm welcome.

"Father wants me to go with you to town," Nolan said. "My friend needs a lift there too." He gestured to the Queen. "But we need to go at once – I'll explain on the way."

"Sounds good to me," Valen said. "The more the merrier."

Before long, they were all seated in the cart with five large sacks of grain stacked behind them. Obie set off at a steady pace, jostling them against each other as the cart trundled along the high hill pass towards town. The haze had burned off, leaving the sky bright and clear. Nolan was surprised to feel a pleasant glow of warmth at being home after so long away. He quickly told Valen everything, being careful not to mention Aroha's true identity.

"It's hard to believe a Beast would come to Mylantis," Valen said, frowning, once Nolan had finished. "Nothing ever happens here."

Running his gaze over the scattered,

sleepy homesteads and terraced fields all around them, Nolan had to agree. There was no sign of trouble. The only news that mattered in Mylantis was the changing price of wheat.

"We swap our grain for flour to make bread," Nolan told Aroha. "Sometimes we have some money to buy meat and butter. These are our last sacks from this harvest, but we should still get a reasonable price. And we can tell the miller, Master Arun, about the Beast. He's the closest thing we have to a mayor, and he can warn the town."

As they travelled onwards, Nolan began to notice darkened patches in some of the fields on either side. The patches became more frequent, and,

passing close to the edge of a terrace, Nolan saw that much of the wheat, which should have been green, was blackened with rot. In the distance,  he spotted tendrils of eerie yellow fog rolling in over the fields.

"What's wrong with the crops?"

Nolan asked Valen. "And what's that strange fog?"

Valen shrugged. "I don't know," he said. "It wasn't like this last time I came by. It looks bad, though. Father will want to know about it."

Gazing at the blighted crops, Aroha frowned. "It doesn't look natural," she said. "Can we go any faster?"

Valen flicked the reins, urging Obie to a reluctant trot, and before long, they reached the sharp descent towards town. Buildings with whitewashed walls and terracotta rooftops nestled in the crook of the valley. Even from way up in the hills Nolan could see the broad road in the middle of the town, heaving with traffic. Market stalls crowded the square at the far end, overlooked by the mill with its huge white sails turning slowly in the breeze. There was no sign of any Beast, and the strange fog hadn't reached the town. In fact, everything looked completely normal.

Obie clopped onwards, carrying them through cobbled lanes, past houses with painted shutters and window boxes full of flowers. As they neared the centre of town, the streets became clogged with carts and shoppers, and they were forced to slow their pace. They eventually reached the busy hubbub of Mill Street, where butchers and bakers

called out their wares and street
hawkers lifted reams of bright
cloth and trinkets as they passed.
Children shouted and laughed,
playing between the stalls, and
street kitchens belched steam from
cauldrons of stew, scenting the air
with spices.

Nolan cursed inwardly as Mill
Street opened into the bustling
market square. Inns and counting
houses surrounded the space, and at
the far end, a queue of carts snaked
towards the mill. Master Arun stood
at the head of the queue behind a
counting table, barking orders at his
men. It looked like there would be a
long wait, but Arun was well known

for his temper. Nolan knew better than to cut into the line.

Valen pulled Obie to a halt at the end of the queue. Queen Aroha sat tensely, her eyes on the fields beyond the town where tattered clouds of yellow mist were starting to coil gently upwards. Nolan chewed his lip. A Beast could attack at any moment!

When they finally reached the front of the queue, Valen leapt from his seat, and Nolan and Aroha handed down the hefty grain sacks.

Arun, barrel-chested and with a starched white tunic stretched tightly over his gut, tugged at his moustache.

"Is that all you've got?" he asked Valen, sneering down at the sacks. "I don't know why you even bothered coming all this way. I'll give you one sack of flour. That's the best I can do."

"It was two bags of grain for one last time we came!" Valen protested.

"I'm not a charity," Master Arun snapped. "I've got to make a profit! If you don't like my prices, you can take your grain elsewhere." This was unfair – there was no other mill. But Nolan had more important things on his mind.

"Master Arun," he called, hopping down from the cart. "I need you to warn the town, and the farmers too.

There's terrible danger coming to Mylantis. A Beast!"

Master Arun blinked and did a double-take. Then he burst out laughing.

"A Beast!" Master Arun said, wiping a fake tear of mirth from his eye. "So, you've finally cracked. I always told your father you would." Aroha leapt from the cart, her armour clanking and her spear gripped tightly in one hand. Arun scowled. "Take my offer before it gets worse."

Aroha stepped forwards until she was almost nose to nose with Arun.

"You, sir, are a fool and a bully!" she said. "Nolan has come all the way from Pania to warn and protect you, and all you can do is laugh?"

Master Arun stiffened, his face darkening as he lifted a meaty finger and jabbed it towards the Queen.

"I will not be spoken to in that way," he growled. "In fact, I'll take that fancy chain you're wearing in compensation for your rudeness!"

Aroha brandished her spear. "I'd like to see you try!" she hissed.

Master Arun balled a fist, but at the same instant, Aroha's spear whipped out, sweeping low, and knocked the miller's legs out from under him. He landed on his backside with a thump. As Master Arun struggled up, huffing and puffing, he called out, "Men!"

Nolan's heart sank as Liam and Mo bustled forwards to stand behind their master. The twins were huge and muscular, and so alike you could only tell them apart by their scars. Mo had a badly set broken nose, and Liam a chunk missing from one ear. They both wielded heavy clubs. Two more men stormed from the mill as well, both brandishing long, curved knives.

"No!" Nolan cried, stepping forwards with his scythe as the men surrounded Aroha. But it was too late. She'd already cracked one over the head with the shaft of her spear. Mo and Liam grabbed her arms and yanked her roughly towards the mill.

"You can't!" Nolan cried, turning his scythe to use it as a lance. He jabbed it at Aroha's nearest captor, but before his blow could connect, something heavy thudded into the back of his skull, and everything exploded in a burst of pain...

3

PLANNING A RESCUE

"Nolan! Wake up!"

Nolan could hear Valen calling him from what seemed like a long way away. His head throbbed and when he tried to open his eyes, sunlight stabbed into his brain. Then everything flooded back to him.

Aroha! Nolan blinked the grogginess from his vision, and Valen's worried face swam into focus.

"Where's the Queen?"

Valen jerked back. "The what?"

"Aroha is the Queen of Tangala," said Nolan. "No joke. We have to rescue her."

Valen frowned. "Oh dear, you must have really hurt your head... They took your friend inside," he said, pointing towards the mill, which was now a fair distance away. Arun and his thugs had gone, and the few remaining carts were dispersing. "I pulled you over here to keep you safe."

Though grateful to his brother, Nolan groaned.

"I'll go and fetch Riko and Boras," Valen said.

"There's no time. We have to do this ourselves. Now, before they harm her."

"How?" Valen asked.

Nolan knitted his brows, trying to make his fuzzy brain work. Then his eyes fell on two unhitched carts outside the mill, one carrying a load of empty hessian sacks. *We need a diversion*, he thought – and with that the outlines of a plan came to him. He shared it with Valen, who grinned. "Dangerous, but it might work…"

Using the wood shavings and flint from his tinder-box, it didn't take Nolan long to set the floury sacks alight. Once he had a good blaze going, Nolan jumped down and nodded to his brother. "Now!" he said, then ducked down behind a water trough.

Valen bent his muscular shoulder to the cart and shoved, smoke rising from the sacks as he wheeled them towards the mill.

"Fire! Help! Fire!" Valen cried, butting the cart up against the wall. "Fire!" he shouted once again, then turned and sped away. Just as Nolan had hoped, Arun and his goons burst from the mill, carrying buckets of sand.

Nolan leapt from his hiding place while the men's backs were turned, and raced into the cool gloom of the mill. The dusky space was alive with creaks and groans, the movement of grinding stone and wooden gears. Hearing a furious, muffled yell,

he spotted Aroha in a shadowy corner, her armour glinting as she struggled. Dropping to her side, Nolan found her hands and feet were tightly bound

and a filthy gag covered her mouth. He sliced her bonds with the blade of his scythe, and Aroha snatched the gag from her mouth.

"Are you hurt?" Nolan asked the Queen.

"Only my pride," she said ruefully. "But it was worth it to see that bully fall in the dust. Let's get out of here."

Peering around the edge of the doorway, Nolan saw that Arun and his men were still putting out the last smouldering embers on the cart. Valen was nowhere to be seen.

"We should head to my father's house," he said. "If we tell him the truth – the whole truth… I'm sure he will help."

Aroha looked as if she was going to argue, but instead, she smiled wearily. "I suppose you're right," she said. "If the worst comes to the worst, I can always command him to evacuate the village by Royal Decree."

A moment later, they were both racing across the square, their boots pounding over the cobbles as they dodged stalls and shoppers loaded down with baskets of goods. But they had only just reached

the centre of the square when a vile yellow mist billowed towards them, carrying the stench of rotting flesh. Nolan slapped a hand over his nose, gagging. A horse let out a piercing whinny and a chorus of terrified screams erupted ahead. Peering through the mist, Nolan could see people dropping their baskets and breaking into panicked runs, scattering produce in every direction. Stall owners ducked behind their counters and children ran screaming into their parents' arms. Horses reared. There was chaos everywhere.

And, at the heart of it, a vast, dark shape loomed in the mist. Nolan and

Aroha both skidded to a halt as the putrid fumes churned, revealing the menace that lurked inside. Every hair on Nolan's head stood on end.

A colossal snake-like monster with tattered frills running the length of her rough-scaled body was slithering towards them. A red tongue flickered between pointed teeth that were coated with venomous spittle.

"The Beast!" Aroha cried.

ENTER DRAKA

The enormous snake reared up, her cold, reptilian gaze fixed on Nolan and Aroha. Then, with a furious hiss, she spat twin streams of white venom from her fangs.

"Run!" Aroha cried. Nolan was already staggering backwards away from the massive snake. His heel landed on the mushy remains of a fruit and he skidded, just catching his balance as the venom hit the cobbles ahead. *SPLAT!* With a bubbling, fizzing sound, the stone dissolved, sending up more clouds of smoke that stung Nolan's eyes. The vile stench of rotting meat hit him like a punch, making him retch.

"This way!" Aroha croaked, one arm flung across her face as she pointed to a narrow gap between two buildings. Nolan raced for cover. Empty barrels from the Miller's Tavern crowded the space, which was too cramped for the Beast to follow. Hugging the wall, Nolan and Aroha coughed and wiped their smarting eyes. From the square, they could hear screaming and shouting and panicked hooves. Above it all came the furious, spine-chilling hiss of the Beast.

"That venom dissolved stone," Nolan wheezed. "How can we fight against that?"

"The same way we fight any Beast," Aroha said. "With steel." She raised her spear, a fierce light in her eyes. Nolan brandished his scythe, feeling a tingling warmth spread up his arms – the magical energy of Tom's Golden Armour.

"Ready?" Aroha asked.

Nolan took a deep breath. He had the Warrior Queen of Tangala at his side and the magical strength of a hero. If he wasn't ready now, he never would be. He nodded. "Ready!"

But, before Nolan and Aroha could leap from their hiding place, a tremendous thud rang out from above, followed by a crash. Nolan ducked as splintered shards of wood and broken roof tiles rained down all around them, clattering off Aroha's armour. A heavy chunk thudded into Nolan's shoulder sending a jolt of pain down his arm. Glancing up, he saw the snake-Beast had rammed the tavern, cracking it open like an egg. A damaged section of wall bulged outwards, swaying...

"Run!" he shouted. Grabbing Aroha's arm, Nolan dragged her into the open just as the wall crashed down, spewing an avalanche of dust and debris after them. Through a clearing in the smog, Nolan saw the Beast strike out after a runaway horse

and cart. The giant snake snapped her jaws shut on the cart, tearing a chunk of wood away, crushing it to matchsticks. The horse reared, wrenching free from its harness, and thundered out of sight. An instant later, Valen burst from a tattered cloud of yellow smoke with Arun and the twins right on his trail.

"Get back here, boy!" Arun shouted. "You'll pay for the damage." But then the mill owner pulled up short as the Beast's huge head snapped around and she fixed him with her gaze.

The three men turned and pelted away, back towards the mill. The Beast surged after them, while Valen stood rooted to the spot, his eyes wide and glassy.

Nolan rushed to his brother. "Are you hurt?" he asked. Valen blinked and turned towards him, his face a blank mask of terror.

"I never thought Draka was real!"

"Draka?" Nolan asked.

"The flying snake-Beast," Valen said. "I thought she was just a story Mum used to tell."

"I don't remember," Nolan said sadly. Then his heart lurched as he fully processed what Valen had said. "Wait! Did you say 'flying'?" Cold dread washed over him as he peered from behind the cart.

Draka was still pursuing Arun and the twins, ramming stalls aside with her blunt-nose and spitting venom as she went. Nolan didn't much like the mill owner, but he couldn't stand by and do nothing.

Swallowing his terror, Nolan rose. "Draka! Over here!" he shouted.

Draka's head snapped around.

Nolan ducked back behind the cart before she could spot him. An instant later, Arun and his thugs finally reached the mill, dived inside and slammed the door.

From his vantage point, Nolan saw Draka hiss with frustration, running her gaze over what was left of the market square. Stall owners crouched behind their shattered counters and shoppers huddled in doorways, too terrified to move.

"Should we mount an attack?" Nolan whispered to the Queen.

Aroha nodded. "If we charge together, we'll have a better chance of success." But suddenly, a hideous noise, like a thousand blades being unsheathed at once, split the air. Nolan gasped to see all the frills along the Beast's sides had flicked open. Flapping them with a hideous clatter like a monstrous clockwork insect, Draka climbed into the air.

The Beast swooped low, firing venom left and right as she went. Every now and then, she flicked her tail, upending barrels of goods, and slashing awnings. Nolan saw the people of Mylantis huddling in fear.

This is my home. . . These are my people!

"I've got to stop her," Nolan told Valen and Aroha. Without giving them time to argue, he charged towards the Beast.

Draka didn't spot Nolan. She continued her mindless rampage, spitting and thrashing her tail. Nolan dodged past puddles of venom and leapt over piles of debris. Sickening yellow fumes rolled over him in waves, burning his throat and making his eyes stream, but he sprinted onwards, drawing closer to the flying snake. Suddenly, her head swivelled around, and her eyes locked with his. Nolan's heart leapt as she dived towards him, but he raced on, hurling himself right beneath her. He felt the down-blast from Draka's clattering wings slam into him, almost knocking him off-balance. He managed to keep his footing and lifted his scythe as high as he could, swiping at her scales. But even at full stretch, he couldn't land a blow.

Queen Aroha reached his side as the Beast sped overhead. She lifted her sword, ready to strike, but Draka had already turned and was coming in for another pass. As Aroha swung her sword, a gust from Draka's wings took it from her grip, sending the weapon off course. It clattered harmlessly to the ground while the Beast spat deadly venom, right towards Nolan.

He dived behind a broken wagon and heard the splat of venom hitting the cobbles nearby. The stench of rotting meat made his head swim. Bile rose in his throat. Forced down on to his hands and knees by sickness, Nolan retched until his stomach was empty. *This is hopeless,* he thought. *I'm hopeless. I can barely stand, let alone fight! Maybe Daltec made a mistake sending a simple farm boy here...* Wiping the sickness from his mouth, Nolan stole a glance from behind the wagon.

Queen Aroha had retrieved her

sword and was running towards Draka once more. Valen had picked up a plank and was holding it like a club. Nolan drew on all his courage and strength and rushed to join them. But, as he raced towards Valen and the Queen, Draka dived, swooping low, her stubby wings creating a deafening, rattling clamour. Torn awnings and fallen produce were whisked into the air beneath the Beast. Ahead, Valen and Aroha staggered as if hit by a tidal wave, both driven to their knees. A powerful gust snatched the breath from Nolan's throat and pelted him with grit. He braced himself, but it was all he could do to keep hold of his scythe as he was thrown to the

ground, rubble thudding into his shoulders and back. As Draka darted overhead she hissed with triumph.

Winded and bruised, Nolan heaved himself up to see the Beast already circling back, more debris swirling in deadly tornadoes below her.

"Valen! Aroha!" he cried as they

staggered up. "This way!" Nolan pointed towards a heavy wagon that lay on its side, then dived behind it. Aroha and Valen joined him. They were barely sheltered from the wind as roof tiles and chunks of masonry smashed against their hiding place.

"What now?" Aroha asked. Her face was grey with dust, and she had a gash along one cheek. A huge bruise bloomed on Valen's forehead and his eyes were round with horror.

"I don't know," Nolan said, panicking. "I don't know!" He heard a calm voice in his ear.

"Don't lose hope." He turned to see the faintest outline of a ghostly figure. *Tom!*

HELP FROM THE MASTER

"What do I do?" Nolan asked Tom. "I can't even reach the Beast, let alone fight her."

Tom smiled sadly, his eyes gentle and kind. "Don't forget, you were chosen for this Quest," he told Nolan. "You earned the right to be here."

"But everything I've tried so far

has failed," Nolan said. "I couldn't convince my own father to believe me." He held out his scythe. "My weapon was useless just now. It was bad enough when Draka was on the ground, but now she can fly…" Nolan trailed off, a wave of hopelessness washing over him.

Tom was still smiling. "You have the perfect weapon," he said.

Nolan shook his head. "Maybe if I were above her," he said. "But that's not going to happen. She's destroying everything."

"There is one way," Tom said, his voice so faint now, Nolan had to strain to hear him. "Magic has always helped me on my Quests. It can help you too. I'll give you my eagle feather."

Nolan gasped as Tom took the shield from his back. He had grown up hearing tales of the magical tokens, and the powers they held – but Nolan never thought he might wield one himself. Tom unclipped the feather and held it out.

"Take it now," Tom said. "I don't have long. Since Malvel cursed me,

I've felt my spirit weakening. Once I give this to you, I don't think I'll be able to take this form again."

"Then I can't take it!" Nolan cried.

"You must!" Tom said. "If the Beast wins, then all is lost. You need this magic. Tangala needs this magic."

"Do as Tom tells you," Aroha said gently. "He has always put his duty first – above everything else. And so must you."

Swallowing a painful lump in his throat, Nolan reached for the feather, unsure what would happen. As his fingertips touched its dim outline, he felt a sharp prickling on his skin, and the feather vanished. A warm tingle flowed up Nolan's arm and through his body, right to the tips of his toes and the top of his head. Then it was gone. Looking up, Nolan realised Tom had gone too.

Before Nolan could say anything, a terrific crash rang out from somewhere nearby and a new cascade of grit and rubble slammed into the cart. Glancing out from his hiding place, Nolan saw a gigantic hole had been punched in the bakery wall, revealing all the ovens inside. A group of villagers burst out, wielding knives, burning torches, pots and pans – anything they could grab. The Beast whipped up another tornado with her wings, throwing the villagers against each other and snatching the makeshift weapons from their hands. One man tumbled to the ground and another fell on top of him. A chunk of brick hit a young woman in the gut, doubling her over in pain. *They'll perish if I don't help them.*

"Nolan!" Valen said, shocking him from his thoughts. "Did Tom's magic work?"

"I guess it's time to find out!" Nolan said.

DESPERATE TIMES

As Nolan burst into the open, he drew back his weapon. "Run!" he screamed to the villagers, then he threw himself headlong at the Beast's scaled back, covering the ground in long strides. The villagers fled into the damaged bakery and Draka, hissing with rage, drew her head back to ram it again. But before she could strike

the building, Nolan bent his knees,
gathered every last shred of strength
he had and jumped.

He swung his scythe overhead in
an arc, using its momentum to carry
him further…and just managed to

slam it into
the Beast's
tail. The jolt
almost tore
the scythe
from Nolan's
hands, but
he hung tight
to the shaft
and heaved
himself
upwards,

gripping the Beast's slippery tail with
both knees. Nolan yanked his scythe
free and swung it again, thudding it
into the Beast's scales, then hauled
himself further up her back.

Draka spat and lashed her tail,
trying to throw Nolan clear, but
he gritted his teeth and, using his
scythe like a grappling hook in one
hand, clawed himself higher with the
fingertips of his other hand. But the
further he climbed, the thicker the
Beast's body became. Soon he could
no longer grip on with his knees. He
crawled instead, hacking his scythe
deep into Draka's scales as she bucked
and thrashed beneath him. Draka
hissed again, craning her head around

fixing him with her reptilian gaze. Nolan saw a flicker of emotion in her eyes – amusement, perhaps. Then she whipped her tail, making her whole body ripple in one long, powerful wave. Nolan's stomach flipped as his scythe lost its purchase and he was tossed upwards, into the air…

BOOF! He hit the ground in a clumsy roll, the hard cobbles punching the breath from lungs. His scythe flew from his grip, and he scrambled after it, but his movements were clumsy and slow. His head was spinning.

"Over here, worm!" Aroha cried. Blinking his dizziness away, Nolan saw the Queen brandishing her sword, waving it at the Beast. Draka's head

whipped around and she spat venom.
Aroha dodged, and the venom hit the
ground where it fizzed and smoked.
"Is that the best you can do?" the
Queen taunted.

Taking the chance Aroha had given
him, Nolan snatched up his weapon.

It had come to rest by the mill, and seeing the building's white flags turning against the blue sky, Nolan had an idea.

Glancing back, he saw Aroha dodge another spurt of venom. Valen ran from his hiding place, waving his makeshift club. Hovering above them, the Beast began to whip her wings in their deadly rhythm, stirring up fallen debris. Nolan knew he didn't have long if he wanted to save his brother and the Queen.

Wrenching the mill door open, Nolan darted inside and made for the rickety steps at the back.

"Hey! Get out of here!" Arun shouted. He and the twins were

hiding down between sacks of flour. Nolan ignored them and hurtled up the wooden steps to the next level. Here, two great mill stones turned with a grating rasp as wooden gears creaked overhead. Nolan took the next flight two steps at a time, reaching a smaller room filled with grain bins. From outside he could hear Draka's wings beating with their hideous clamour.

Nolan kept going, up the final set of steps to a tiny room with an upright wheel set in the floor. Here the creaking and groaning of the mill's insides almost drowned out the wind. Nolan rushed to the window, shoved it open and peered out. Draka hovered below him, her wings whipping in circles, creating a spinning column of air filled with debris. And caught in the centre of the tornado, whirling around and around, was Valen! Aroha tried to reach him, but each time she drew close, the wind buffeted her away.

"Let my brother go!" Nolan roared. He climbed from the window, hurling himself towards the Beast. He landed on her back in a crouch, just behind her huge, blunt head. Sensing the impact, Draka's wingbeats faltered, and with the sudden dip of the wind, Valen staggered free of the tornado and Aroha tugged him to safety.

Time to strike the killing blow!
Nolan stood and lifted his scythe,
ready to drive it hard into the base
of Draka's skull. But, at that instant,
Draka swooped skywards, her scales
whipping out from under his feet.
For a heartbeat, he plummeted, but
then a terrific wind snatched him up
and spun him around like a feather
on the breeze.

Nolan could hear Draka's
wingbeats from below him now – she
must have turned a full loop – but
with everything whirling around
him, he could hardly see... Then
suddenly, he glimpsed Draka's open
jaws, her curved fangs, only an arm's
reach away. *She's going to swallow*

me! Panic ignited his blood, and Nolan swung his scythe, hoping the magical powers of Tom's armour

would guide his strike. He felt the blow connect, chopping off a fang with a sharp crack! But he had no time to celebrate. Draka hissed, and the roar of her wingbeats became deafening. A powerful gust slammed into Nolan from below and his stomach lurched as he was catapulted upwards, high into the air. The sails of the windmill flashed past him but still he climbed, higher and higher until the market square was spread below him. Terror squeezed Nolan's heart as he slowed, then felt a downward tug on his gut.

He was falling to his death.

FEATHERS AND FLOUR

Fighting hard to control his panic,
Nolan pictured Tom's eagle feather
in his mind's eye…and as soon as he
did, a sudden lightness enveloped
him. All at once, instead of falling, he
was swooping smoothly downwards.
Below him, the Beast thrashed wildly,
her long tail whipping as she shot

91

venom at everything in sight. Plumes of vile-smelling smoke billowed upwards, hiding much of the square. But, keeping his eyes locked on the raging reptile, Nolan found he could angle his body to direct his path. *I'm flying!* As Nolan swooped lower, he picked up speed. Holding his scythe high and bracing himself against the impact, he aimed directly for the Beast.

Just before he slammed into the back of Draka's head, Nolan swung his scythe. THUD! With his full weight behind it, the blade drove deep into the Beast's scales.

Draka lashed her head from side to side, spitting madly, trying to shake

Nolan off. His bones and teeth rattled, but Nolan held tight to his weapon with both hands and let his body go slack – becoming a dead weight. The blade of his scythe ripped through the Beast's flesh as Nolan slid down her back, tearing a long gash. Blue blood welled from the cut and Draka's body shuddered as she let out a gasp of pain. Bracing his feet against the Beast's scales, Nolan yanked his blade free just as he reached one of her stubby wings. Then, using the last of his momentum, he hacked at the wing, slicing a piece off. Finally, Nolan flung himself away from Draka and hit the ground in a crouch. Above him, the huge snake raged, beating her wings fiercely, the injured one hanging limp. She turned and swooped overhead, careening off at a crazy angle – heading straight for the mill – unable to direct her flight.

CRASH! The Beast's head ploughed into the building, punching a great hole in the brickwork. White clouds of flour filled the air, obscuring everything. Then the Beast rose from the debris, flapping clumsily away, fat drops of blue blood trailing from her wounds. A moment later, shadowy figures moved in the whiteness of the mill.

"Help! I can't see!" someone cried. Nolan recognised the panicked voice as Arun's. The twins were there too,

stumbling, their arms flailing blindly as they emerged from the wreckage of the mill.

"This way!" Nolan called, grabbing Arun's arm and tugging him away from the building. The twins, coughing and wiping their eyes, stumbled after them. All three of them were covered head to toe with flour.

"Nolan!" Aroha said, her voice full of relief as she arrived. "That was incredible!"

Valen's eyes looked enormous in his flour-covered face. "What do we do now?" he asked Nolan and the Queen. "The Beast has fled."

"She'll be back," said Nolan grimly.

"Well, I'm not giving up, that's for

sure," Aroha said. "I'll see this Quest through if it kills me." From the angle of her jaw and the icy fire in her gaze, Nolan knew Aroha's words were true – and they terrified him. *I can't let the Queen of Tangala die!* He lifted his own chin and stood tall.

"I won't let it come to that," Nolan said. "I can attack from the air again and cut off another wing."

"But the mill's barely standing," Aroha said. "And that last attack almost killed you. It's too risky."

As Nolan took in the devastation all around him, his shoulders sagged. Flour drifted slowly downwards, covering smashed stalls and scattered produce – the livelihoods of his neighbours all destroyed. He felt suddenly exhausted, right to his core. From somewhere nearby, he heard the wingbeats of the Beast start up again and his heart sank even further. After everything he had done, Draka was still as strong as ever.

"It's my job to defeat her," he said. "I need to come up with a plan!"

"We're here, boy!" a rasping voice called from behind Nolan. He turned to see three more figures emerge from the fog of flour – one bent, the other two broad-shouldered.

"Father!" Nolan cried.

"The baker told us what happened," Riko said, brandishing a hoe in one hand and a threshing flail in the other.

"We've come to help," Boras added, armed the same way.

Dillan struck the ground with his cane, his eyes fierce and his jaw set. "That snake is going to regret she ever came to Mylantis!" he said. Nolan grinned. With his whole family working together, surely they couldn't fail!

1

8

BLIND FAITH

"Thank you for coming to our aid,"
Aroha said to Nolan's father and
brothers. "Once this is all over,
the palace shall richly repay your
bravery."

"The palace!" Dillan cried as the
penny dropped. "I had a feeling you
weren't just any old warrior. Who
are you?"

"The Queen of Tangala," Aroha said with a grin.

Riko and Boras quickly dropped to their knees. Even Dillan dipped his head a little.

Aroha rolled her eyes. "We don't have time for this. Now, get up, and let's finish the Quest!"

Riko and Boras rose. "What's the

plan?" Riko asked.

"Yes, how are you going to save what's left of my mill?" Arun added, still rubbing at his gummy eyes. Nolan had been about to admit he didn't know, but the sight of Master Arun's grimy white face and the twins both scrubbing at their eyes gave him an idea.

"Flour!" he exclaimed.

Dillan narrowed his eyes. "Flour?" he said. "That doesn't sound like a plan."

"We'll use flour against the Beast," Nolan said, his thoughts racing now. "Everyone fetch a sack from the mill and hide with them behind that cart." He pointed to an upturned wagon nearby. "I'll draw the Beast in, and when I give the signal, throw the flour over her. She won't be able to see – and that will give me the chance I need to defeat her."

"Now that sounds more like a plan," Dillan said, nodding his approval. "A crazy one, but I like it. Let's do it!"

A sudden angry hiss reached them, followed by a snap of wings. Everyone jolted into action. Nolan's family and Aroha all raced into the ruined mill. Even the twins joined them.

Nolan lifted his scythe. His whole body was thrumming with nervous energy, but he held his weapons steady and strode off in the opposite direction, towards the Beast.

"I'm over here!" Nolan called once he had put a good distance between himself and the mill. Through the murky clouds of flour and putrid fog, he could just make out Draka's huge form flapping crookedly towards him. He set off at an angle, waving his scythe as he ran, hoping she would follow – and soon he heard her beating wingbeats on his trail. His heart pounded in his chest, but Nolan kept going, expecting at any moment to feel the burning sting of the Beast's venom on his back. He dodged between smashed stalls and wrecked carts, weaving back towards the mill. And suddenly, almost too soon, the towering shape of the mill loomed before him. *I hope they're ready!* Glancing towards the upturned cart, Nolan spied the tops of his brothers' heads peeking from behind it, then a glint of armour as Aroha raised an arm, giving him the thumbs up.

Now it's down to me! Nolan pulled to a halt and turned. The Beast's vast scaled form powered towards him, the din from her wings drowning out any other sound. Nolan stood his ground and tossed his weapon aside. As the scythe clattered to the cobbles, Draka's eyes narrowed to spiteful slits and her jaws spread wide in what looked like an eager grin. Nolan's knees shook and his heart quailed, but he didn't move – not until Draka filled his whole view, her fangs dripping venom.

"NOW!" Nolan roared, throwing himself to the ground on his belly. Draka hissed in rage, but carried by her own momentum, she couldn't stop. As her body whipped overhead, darkening the day, Nolan snatched up his fallen weapon. He turned just in time to see Aroha and the rest of his family hurl the contents of their flour sacks over the Beast. Draka slammed into the damaged wall of the mill with a thunderous crash, then turned, whipping her head from side to side. Clouds of flour swirled around him, but Nolan could make out Draka's

head,
covered
in the
stuff. She
writhed
and
shook,
spitting
and
flapping
in fury
and panic, her huge eyes milky white,
blinded by flour. Unbalanced by her
torn wing, she lurched sideways and
crashed into the wall of the counting
house. The heavy door lintel fell,
smashing her to the ground, yet still
she thrashed and twisted. More of

the building crumbled on top of her, burying her in huge chunks of fallen masonry. Draka's panicked movements began to slow. The clattering of her wings fell silent, and for an instant, everything was still.

Nolan picked his way through the rubble. Draka lay amid the debris, her sides heaving and the long wound along her body oozing with blue blood. Her tongue flicked in and out with each laboured breath, and her eyes were sticky with a doughy gum.

Nolan felt a stab of pity at the sight. Draka's rasping breaths were panicked and fast. Shudders of pain wracked her form.

"I do not want to kill you," Nolan

said, not knowing if she would understand. Her head lifted a little, turning towards him. "You must submit and give me the token. Then you must leave this place for good."

Draka let out a vicious hiss, and her head whipped out. Nolan stumbled back and fell. For a moment, the great fanged head towered over him, ready to strike. But suddenly the Beast's body gave a mighty spasm and a wet rasp of pain tore from her throat. Her head flopped lifelessly to the ground and her eyes closed. Sitting up, Nolan saw Queen Aroha standing beside the Beast, her sword driven deep into Draka's scales at the base of her neck. Nolan saw a sadness in her eyes.

"Draka left me no choice," she said. "She would have brought death and destruction to this region and beyond, if I hadn't…" She grimaced and looked away for a moment.

"Thank you, Your Majesty," Nolan breathed. He stood up, feeling suddenly cold and a little sad at the mighty form lying dead before him. His head dipped in grief.

Aroha wiped her eyes and pulled her weapon free. "You have a good heart," she told him. "It is right that you should take no pleasure from the death of a Beast. It will serve you well on all your Quests – which I feel will be many."

Nolan lifted his eyes and managed a

smile. "I hope so," he said.

The queen walked with him back out into the wreckage of the square, where his brothers greeted him with a cheer.

Riko grinned. "That was seriously impressive!"

Boras smiled too. "No more teasing about your plans to become a hero. You already are one!" he said. Suddenly his head snapped up, and Nolan heard the clatter of shifting rubble from behind him.

"What do you think you're doing?" Riko demanded. Turning around, Nolan spotted Arun creeping from the ruins of the counting house, something concealed behind his back.

"And what are you holding?" Dillan demanded. "Looting is a crime, you know?"

Arun sheepishly held the thing out – it looked like a shiny red tile. "It fell off the Beast's back," he said. "I thought I should take it as payment for the damage done to my mill."

Nolan strode forwards and held out his hand. "Give it to me," he said. "It is mine, and I need it to save Tom's life." Arun scowled and looked like he was about to refuse, until Valen and Queen Aroha stepped to Nolan's sides. The miller handed the scale over and Nolan tucked it safely into his tunic.

"We've done it!" Nolan said, once

Arun had skulked away.

"You did it, son," Dillan told him. "I am sorry I've always been so hard on you. I wanted you to help look after the farm, but it seems you have a whole kingdom to look after. I'm proud of you, boy." Nolan blinked hard, a tear running from his left eye.

"Are you ready to return to Pania?" Aroha asked him. "Daltec has a potion to make with that scale. I just hope the other three Quests have been successful too."

Nolan nodded. "I'm sure they must have been," he said, trying to sound more certain than he felt. Defeating Draka had been far more difficult than he could have imagined. Fears had been nagging at him ever since Tom had given him the eagle feather. Tom had said that his strength was fading fast. Nolan felt cold all over again.

What if it's too late? What if the Master of the Beasts is gone for good?

THE END

CONGRATULATIONS, YOU HAVE COMPLETED THIS QUEST!

At the end of each chapter you were awarded a special gold coin.
The QUEST in this book was worth an amazing 8 coins.

Look at the Beast Quest totem picture opposite to see how far you've come in your journey to become

MASTER OF THE BEASTS.

The more books you read, the more coins you will collect!

Do you want your own
Beast Quest Totem?

1. Cut out and collect the coin below
2. Go to the Beast Quest website
3. Download and print out your totem
4. Add your coin to the totem

www.beastquest.co.uk

READ THE BOOKS, COLLECT THE COINS!
EARN COINS FOR EVERY CHAPTER YOU READ!

550+ COINS
MASTER OF THE BEASTS

550+
515
480
445
410
395
380
365
350
320
290
260
230
217
206
191
180

410 COINS
HERO

350 COINS
WARRIOR

230 COINS
KNIGHT

180 COINS
SQUIRE

44 COINS
PAGE

8 COINS
APPRENTICE

READ ALL THE BOOKS IN SERIES 29:
THE NEW PROTECTORS!

Don't miss the next exciting Beast Quest book: LUKOR THE FOREST DEMON!

Read on for a sneak peek…

THROUGH THE PORTAL

"Ready?" Daltec asked Katya. The portal the wizard had made hung in the air before them, shimmering gold and green like sunlight on water. Katya took one final look back at the throne room where Tom lay unconscious, deadly poison flowing in his veins. *He needs me to succeed!* she thought, tightening her grip on the pommel of her axe. Since being dipped in the molten gold of Tom's gauntlet, the weapon felt lighter

than ever. She tucked it into her belt and nodded firmly.

"Ready!" she replied.

With Daltec at her side, she stepped

through the portal. Her stomach swooped. Flashes of emerald light glimmered all around her, and for an instant, she felt weightless, perfectly suspended. Then, her feet hit the ground. The lights faded to a dusky green, and she found herself standing in the cool dimness of her home forest. Glancing over her shoulder, she watched the portal shrink to a tiny point of light, then vanish.

Daltec was glancing around, frowning uncertainly. "I'm not quite sure where we are," he said. "I'd hoped there'd be a path of some sort."

Katya turned a full circle, taking in the dense foliage, mosses and ferns to get her bearings. "It's all right," she said. "You're not supposed to see the trails. I'll take you to my home – my parents should have noticed if a Beast's been hanging around."

Katya struck off through the twilit forest. The sound of evening birdsong echoed around her and the faint tang of woodsmoke hung in the air. Despite the familiar surroundings, her nerves thrummed, every sense on high alert. They were on a Quest to find a magical token to heal Tom, Avantia's Master of the Beasts, who had been poisoned by the Evil Wizard Malvel. But to obtain the token, each of Tangala's new protectors would have to defeat a Beast.

"Are you sure this is the right way?" asked Daltec.

Katya nodded. "You see this mark?" she said, pointing to a faint cut scored on a nearby tree. "Many of the trees have these – they were made by the Forest Folk, and they're easy to follow if you know how."

Daltec peered closer. "Fascinating!" he said. "I can barely see it even now you've pointed it out."

As they trudged onwards Katya listened hard for any sound that might indicate a Beast, but she heard only the usual creaks and chirps of the forest creatures settling for the night, along with the quiet tread of their own boots. Eventually, though, she heard the dull, repetitive thunk of an axe. Lots of axes.

"The loggers!" she said, balling a fist. "They never used to come this far inside the forest!" The noise grew steadily louder as Katya pushed onwards, her jaw clenched with rage. The trees here were ancient living things, but the loggers were only interested in profit.

"Oi!" a rough voice shouted. "What are you doing here?" A burly man with broad, muscular shoulders swaggered from the undergrowth, wielding a massive two-headed axe.

Katya glared at him. "I live here," she said. "I could ask you the same question."

"I'm here to oversee the logging,"
the man answered.

"Have you no respect!" Katya
growled.

"For what?" the man scoffed. "A girl
and a skinny whelp of a lad?"

"For the trees," said Katya,
gripping the handle of her axe.

The logger laughed.

Daltec put a hand on her arm. "Remember," he said. "We're on a Quest to help Tom. We need to focus."

It took all of Katya's restraint, but she drew a deep breath. "Fine."

The man leered at her. "Now off you go, girlie."

Still seething, Katya stormed away. Once she and Daltec had put some distance between themselves and the logger, Daltec turned to Katya with a puzzled frown. "I thought your father was a logger?" he said.

"My father was a woodcutter," Katya told him. "That's completely different. He's old now, so he's a carpenter. But even before that, he was a skilled artisan, not a tree butcher like—"

A spear whizzed through the air and thudded into the earth at their feet. Daltec sprang back in alarm, but Katya plucked the weapon from the ground, her anger evaporating. She smiled. "You can come out!" Katya called.

A woman stepped out from the undergrowth, wearing a simple tunic.

Read
LUKOR THE FOREST DEMON
to find out what happens next!